INCREDIBLE
SPORTS
RECORDS
★ ★ ★ ★ ★

BASKETBALL

RECORDS

BY THOMAS K. ADAMSON

BLASTOFF!
DISCOVERY

Bellwether Media • Minneapolis, MN

Blastoff! Discovery launches a new mission: reading to learn. Filled with facts and features, each book offers you an exciting new world to explore!

This edition first published in 2018 by Bellwether Media, Inc.

No part of this publication may be reproduced in whole or in part without written permission of the publisher.
For information regarding permission, write to Bellwether Media, Inc., Attention: Permissions Department,
5357 Penn Avenue South, Minneapolis, MN 55419.

Library of Congress Cataloging-in-Publication Data

Names: Adamson, Thomas K., 1970- author.
Title: Basketball Records / by Thomas K. Adamson.
Description: Minneapolis, MN : Bellwether Media, Inc., 2018.
  | Series: Blastoff! Discovery. Incredible Sports Records |
  Includes bibliographical references and index. |
  Audience: Age 7-13. | Audience: Grade 3 to 8.
Identifiers: LCCN 2017032286 (print) |
LCCN 2017032985 (ebook) | ISBN 9781626177826
  (hardcover : alk. paper) | ISBN 9781618913128
  (pbk. : alk. paper) | ISBN 9781681034935 (ebook)
Subjects: LCSH: Basketball–Records–United States–Juvenile
  literature. | National Basketball Association–Juvenile literature.
Classification: LCC GV885.55 (ebook) | LCC GV885.55 .A34
  2018 (print) | DDC 796.323/6406–dc23
LC record available at https://lccn.loc.gov/2017032286

Editor: Nathan Sommer   Designer: Steve Porter

Printed in the United States of America, North Mankato, MN.

TABLE OF CONTENTS

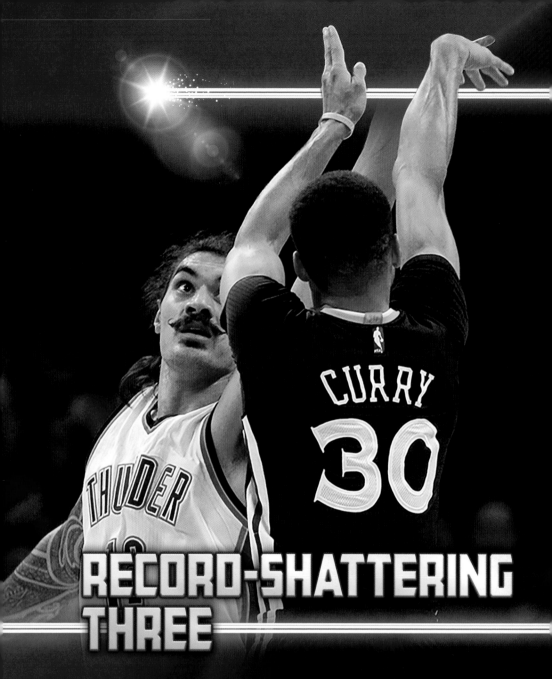

RECORD-SHATTERING THREE

It is February 27, 2016. Golden State Warriors superstar Stephen Curry has the ball. He hops right as he dribbles behind his back. The other team cannot keep up! Curry fires from behind the **3-point line**. Swish! The shot is his record-breaking 287th **3-pointer** of the season.

Curry finishes the season with 402 3-pointers. Rarely are records broken by so much! Feats like this are what fans love about the National Basketball Association (NBA) and Women's National Basketball Association (WNBA). Read on to learn about the most breathtaking basketball records!

RECORD-BREAKING PLAYERS

Players in the NBA and WNBA have earned some awesome records. Many of these **offensive** and **defensive** records once seemed impossible. They are some of basketball's most memorable feats!

Michael Jordan is one of the NBA's all-time greats. His career average of 30.12 points per game is the highest in NBA history. His dominance each year brought the Chicago Bulls six NBA championships!

HIGHEST CAREER AVERAGE POINTS PER GAME, NBA

Record: 30.12 points
Record holder: Michael Jordan
Year record was set: 2003
Former record holder:
Wilt Chamberlain

MOST CAREER ASSISTS, NBA

Record: 15,806 assists
Record holder: John Stockton
Year record was set: 2003
Former record holder:
Magic Johnson

Scoring points is great, but someone has to get the ball to the scorers. The player who helps create a scoring play often gets an **assist**. John Stockton was the best at this. His record of 15,806 assists is more than 3,700 ahead of the next best player!

Few players have ruled the WNBA like Diana Taurasi. Her leadership earned her two **Most Valuable Player** (MVP) awards and three championships with the Phoenix Mercury. It also earned her the league's all-time scoring record in 2017. Her 7,867 career points will be tough to beat!

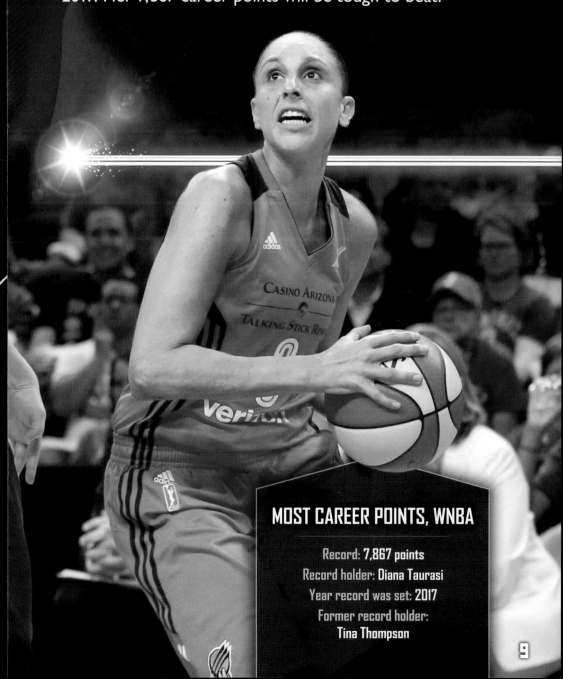

MOST CAREER POINTS, WNBA

Record: 7,867 points
Record holder: Diana Taurasi
Year record was set: 2017
Former record holder:
Tina Thompson

The flashiest NBA records are made on offense. But few have forgotten defensive icon Dikembe Mutombo! He holds the record for most **consecutive** seasons leading the NBA in **blocked shots**. Mutombo would often wag his finger as a warning after each block.

MOST CONSECUTIVE SEASONS LEADING NBA IN BLOCKED SHOTS

Record: 5 seasons
Record holder: Dikembe Mutombo
Year record was set: 1996
Former record holder: Elmore Smith

MOST MVP AWARDS, NBA

Record: 6 MVP awards
Record holder: Kareem Abdul-Jabbar
Year record was set: 1980
Former record holder:
Bill Russell

SCORING GREAT

Abdul-Jabbar also holds the
NBA record for most career
points scored with 38,387.

Kareem Abdul-Jabbar was one of the greatest scorers
and **rebounders** in the NBA. He was the NBA's MVP a
record six times because of this! Abdul-Jabbar also had an
incredible average of playing 78 games per season.

MOST POINTS SCORED, ROOKIE SEASON, NBA

Record: 2,707 points
Record holder: Wilt Chamberlain
Year record was set: 1960
Former record holder: Elgin Baylor

SUPERB ROOKIE SEASON

Chamberlain's other rookie records include most points in a game and most rebounds in a season.

Wilt Chamberlain was unstoppable from the start. He scored 2,707 points during his **rookie** season. This smashed the record for most points scored by a rookie. It was the most points anyone had scored during one season at the time!

Tamika Catchings was one of the WNBA's toughest players. She nabbed a record 3,316 rebounds in her career. Her power and skill on defense earned her five Defensive Player of the Year Awards.

MOST CAREER REBOUNDS, WNBA

Record: 3,316 rebounds
Record holder: Tamika Catchings
Year record was set: 2016
Former record holder: Lisa Leslie

RECORD-BREAKING TEAMS

The best teams use each player's strengths to succeed. When these players work together, they win games and championships. Sometimes they even set records!

The 2015–2016 Golden State Warriors will be hard to forget. Their 73 wins that season were more than any other team in NBA history. This forceful Warriors team started off the year with 24 wins in a row, also a stunning NBA record.

COULDN'T FINISH IT

The Warriors failed to end their record-breaking season with a title. They lost the NBA Finals to the Cleveland Cavaliers.

BEST REGULAR SEASON RECORD, NBA

Record: 73-9
Record holder: Golden State Warriors
Year record was set: 2016
Former record holder: Chicago Bulls

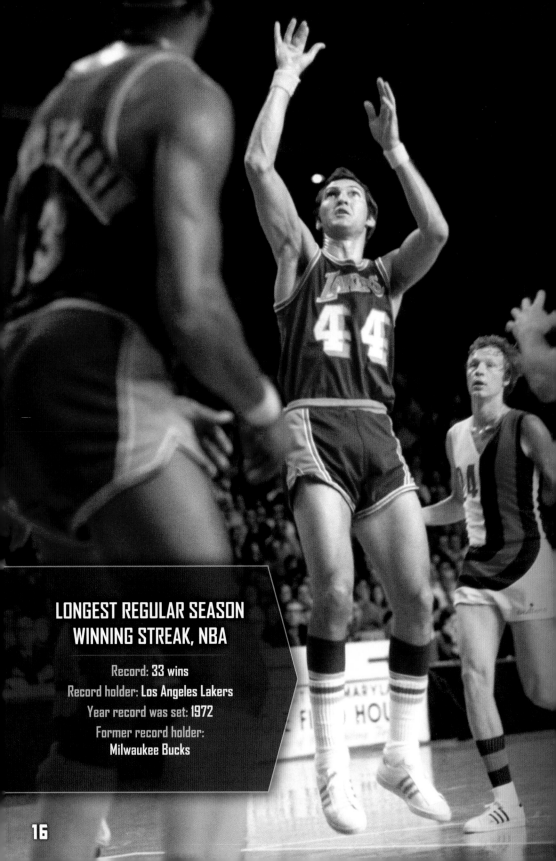

LONGEST REGULAR SEASON WINNING STREAK, NBA

Record: 33 wins
Record holder: Los Angeles Lakers
Year record was set: 1972
Former record holder:
Milwaukee Bucks

The Warriors started a season with 24 wins, but the Los Angeles Lakers still hold the record for the longest win **streak**. Their 1971–1972 team dominated opponents to win 33 games in a row. This excellent team also took home the NBA championship.

In the WNBA, the Phoenix Mercury is one of the most record-breaking teams. Led by superstars like Diana Taurasi and Penny Taylor, the Mercury have often led the WNBA in scoring. In 2010, they did so like never before. The team racked up a record 93.9 points per game that year!

Diana Taurasi

Penny Taylor

HIGHEST AVERAGE POINTS PER GAME, WNBA

Record: 93.9 points
Record holder: Phoenix Mercury
Year record was set: 2010
Former record holder:
broke their own record

It's not always good to break a record. The Philadelphia 76ers learned this the hard way. They hold the record for the NBA's longest losing streak. This 76ers team lost the last ten games of the 2014–2015 season. Then they opened the next with 18 straight losses!

LONGEST LOSING STREAK, NBA

Record: 28 losses
Record holder: Philadelphia 76ers
Year record was set: 2015
Former record holder:
Cleveland Cavaliers

DOMINATING THE DECADE

The Celtics won the championship 11 out of 14 seasons from 1956 to 1969. Bill Russell played during each of these seasons.

Bill Russell

MOST CHAMPIONSHIPS IN A ROW, NBA

Record: 8 championships
Record holder: Boston Celtics
Year record was set: 1966
Former record holder:
Minneapolis Lakers

The Boston Celtics of the 1950s and 1960s are perhaps the most dominant team ever. They won eight straight championships, led by superstar Bill Russell. No other team has ever won more than three in a row!

RECORD-BREAKING GAMES

Fans never know what to expect when they attend a professional basketball game. Any game could end up being remembered forever. Some performances are so unbelievable they set records!

Wilt Chamberlain had an unforgettable game on March 2, 1962. The Philadelphia Warriors **center** scored 100 points against the New York Knicks. Entire teams often fail to score that many points in a game!

Michael Jordan

FIFTY-POINT FEATS

Wilt Chamberlain also holds the record for most 50-point games with 118. Michael Jordan is a distant second with only 31 games!

MOST POINTS SCORED IN A GAME BY ONE PLAYER, NBA

Record: 100 points
Record holder: Wilt Chamberlain
Year record was set: 1962
Former record holder:
Elgin Baylor

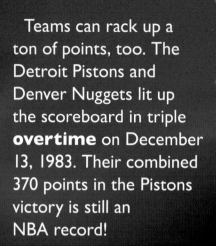

Teams can rack up a ton of points, too. The Detroit Pistons and Denver Nuggets lit up the scoreboard in triple **overtime** on December 13, 1983. Their combined 370 points in the Pistons victory is still an NBA record!

DOUBLE RECORD-BREAKERS!

The Pistons broke more than one scoring record during that game. Their 186 points also remain the most points scored by one team in a game!

MOST COMBINED POINTS, ONE NBA GAME

Record: 370 points
Record holders: Detroit Pistons and Denver Nuggets
Year record was set: 1983
Former record holders: Milwaukee Bucks and San Antonio Spurs

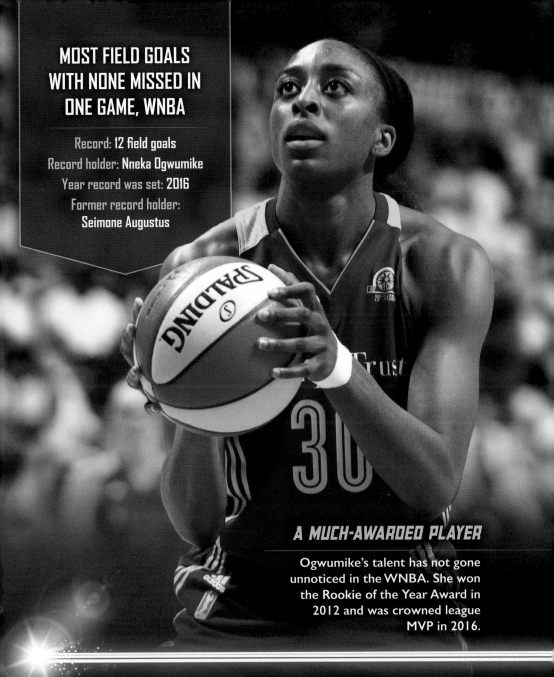

MOST FIELD GOALS WITH NONE MISSED IN ONE GAME, WNBA

Record: 12 field goals
Record holder: Nneka Ogwumike
Year record was set: 2016
Former record holder:
Seimone Augustus

A MUCH-AWARDED PLAYER

Ogwumike's talent has not gone unnoticed in the WNBA. She won the Rookie of the Year Award in 2012 and was crowned league MVP in 2016.

WNBA players cannot hope for a better game than the one Nneka Ogwumike had on June 11, 2016. The Los Angeles Sparks player made all twelve of her **field goal** attempts against the Dallas Wings. It was the most shots without a miss in WNBA history!

FEWEST POINTS SCORED BY ONE TEAM IN AN NBA GAME (SINCE 1954-1955)

Record: 49 points
Record holder: Chicago Bulls
Year record was set: 1999
Former record holder:
Utah Jazz

The Chicago Bulls are not proud of their game on April 10, 1999. Their 49 points against the Miami Heat were the fewest scored ever in an NBA game. They made just 23.4 percent of their shots during this poor performance!

The most exciting shots are often 3-pointers. The Cleveland Cavaliers hit an amazing 25 of them in one game on March 3, 2017. Kyle Korver hit the record-breaking shot against the Hawks with one minute left in the game!

KING JAMES HITS THE SHOTS

LeBron James led the way for the Cavs with six 3-pointers during this game. The Cavs made over half of their attempted 3-point shots as a team.

MOST 3-POINTERS BY A TEAM IN A REGULAR SEASON GAME, NBA

Record: 25 3-pointers
Record holder: Cleveland Cavaliers
Year record was set: 2017
Former record holder:
Houston Rockets

RECORD-BREAKING PLAYS

Sometimes, single plays can make history and shock the world. Fans beg for the magic teams perform on the court. Often, these plays make a player or team live on forever in the record books!

Charlotte Hornets star Baron Davis got the ball with seconds left in the 3rd quarter on February 17, 2001. Davis chucked the ball toward the basket with nothing to lose. His 89-foot (27.1-meter) throw went in, setting the record for longest shot ever made!

LONGEST SHOT MADE, NBA

Record: 89 feet (27.1 meter)
Record holder: Baron Davis
Year record was set: 2001
Former record holder:
Norm Van Lier

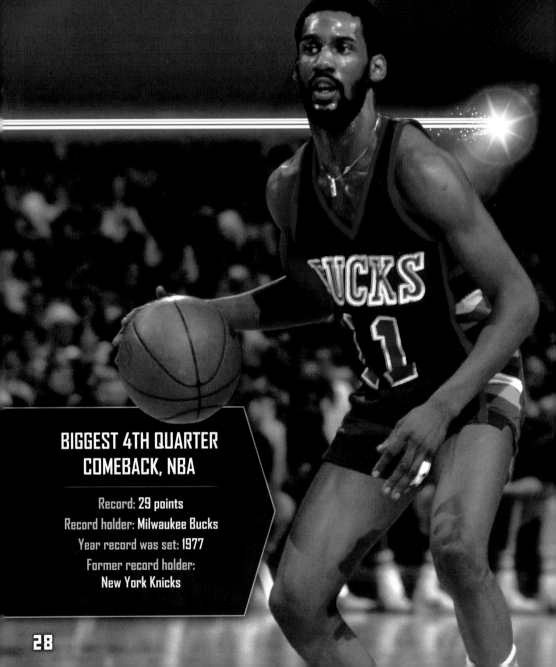

The Milwaukee Bucks were down 29 points with 8:43 left to play on November 25, 1977. But they did not quit. Somehow, the Bucks went on an unthinkable 35–4 run to defeat the Hawks. This remains the largest 4th quarter **comeback** in NBA history.

BIGGEST 4TH QUARTER COMEBACK, NBA

Record: 29 points
Record holder: Milwaukee Bucks
Year record was set: 1977
Former record holder:
New York Knicks

MOST FIELD GOALS, ONE WNBA GAME

Record: 18 field goals
Record holder: Lauren Jackson
Year record was set: 2007
Former record holder:
Cynthia Cooper

A TRULY DOMINANT YEAR

Jackson did not just dominate on offense in 2007. She was also named the WNBA's Defensive Player of the Year and MVP that year.

The Seattle Storm's Lauren Jackson controlled the court against the Washington Mystics on July 24, 2007. With seconds left in overtime, Jackson hit a 3-pointer for her 18th field goal of the game. The Storm lost, but the play earned Jackson the WNBA field goal record.

GLOSSARY

3-point line—the curved line on the court that shows where a shot is worth three points instead of two

3-pointer—a field goal taken from behind a line that counts for three points instead of two

assist—a stat that comes from helping another player score by passing the ball to them

blocked shots—shots that are knocked away by a defender while the ball is in the air

center—a player who plays defense near the hoop; the center is often the tallest or biggest player on the team.

comeback—when a team overcomes a losing score to win a game

consecutive—one right after the other

defensive—relating to the player or team that does not have the ball and is trying to prevent the other team from scoring

field goal—any basket made that is not a free throw

Most Valuable Player—an award given at the end of the season to the most outstanding player of the season; this award is called MVP for short.

offensive—relating to the player or team that has the ball and is trying to score

overtime—extra time added to a game because the score is tied

rebounders—players who get control of the ball after a missed shot

rookie—a first-year professional player

streak—a series of events that happen one right after the other

TO LEARN MORE

AT THE LIBRARY

Aretha, David. *Top 10 Moments in Basketball*. New York, N.Y.: Enslow Publishing, 2017.

Frederick, Shane. *Basketball's Record Breakers*. North Mankato, Minn.: Capstone Press, 2017.

Savage, Jeff. *Basketball Super Stats*. Minneapolis, Minn.: Lerner Publications, 2017.

ON THE WEB

Learning more about basketball records is as easy as 1, 2, 3.

1. Go to www.factsurfer.com.

2. Enter "basketball records" into the search box.

3. Click the "Surf" button and you will see a list of related web sites.

With factsurfer.com, finding more information is just a click away.

INDEX